A Day at the Zo

Hattie and friends

Lesley Berrington

.... For my daughter, Harriet

www.hattieandfriends.com

I S B N 0-9552141-0-6
I S B N 978-0-9552141-0-3

Printed by JW Ruddock and Sons Ltd, Lincoln, England

It was a special day.

Hattie and George were going to visit the zoo and they were so excited.

Hattie's mummy made a picnic with ham sandwiches and chocolate muffins – delicious!

George's mummy brought some sweets for the journey.

'I can't wait to see the elephants,' George said as they went through the big metal gates at the entrance to the zoo.

'Let's find the monkeys first, I love them,' said Hattie.

There were lots of other children already at the zoo.

As they turned the corner they saw a very tall and elegant animal.
She was munching away on juicy green leaves from the tree- tops.
'Wow, look, that giraffe can reach the sky!' said George.
Even the baby giraffe towered above all the children at the zoo.

George was thrilled to see the elephants were nearby.

There were two big grey elephants called Tilly and Jake and their baby called Ellie.

She looked like lots of fun as she sprayed water from her trunk and wriggled and rolled in the dust.

Hattie and George found the penguins next, waddling around their pool.

The penguins slid into the water and swam so easily, chasing each other around under water.

'They look like they're wearing suits, don't they?' laughed George's mummy.

'Time for our picnic.'

Hattie's mummy unpacked the sandwiches, crisps and cheese cubes.
She poured four cups of lemonade and offered the children straws.
George chose a green straw and Hattie chose a purple straw.

'Purple is my favourite colour,' said Hattie.
'And green is my favourite colour,' said George.

Hattie and George thought the best bit about the picnic was the chocolate muffin but it was a bit messy!

Just as they were wiping their faces George's mummy said, 'if we hurry we can see the parrot show, it's starting in the arena at 2 'o' clock.'

The parrots were so clever and their feathers were beautiful colours.

One parrot called 'Mikey' could even ride a bike!

George was very brave when a parrot sat on his shoulder.
It kept saying, 'hello George, hello George.'

Hattie thought it might peck his ear!

'We can find the monkeys now,' Hattie's mummy said after the parrot show.
'Hurray!' shouted Hattie.

The monkeys were swinging, jumping and running about, playing games.

Hattie and George went right up to the glass and one monkey came to make faces at them.
'Cheeky- monkey face!' Hattie giggled.

It was nearly time to leave the zoo but there was just time to visit the 'Reptile House'.

It was very dark and warm inside. There were sleepy snakes and strange looking lizards with long tongues. There was even a big alligator that had very pointy teeth.

Hattie and George didn't stay too long in there!

'Who would like an ice-cream?' Asked George's mummy.

'Me please!' shouted Hattie and George together.

George had a tub of chocolate and strawberry ice cream with sprinkles on top.
Hattie chose an ice-lolly that looked like a spaceship with red, yellow and green stripes.

Hattie and George had really enjoyed their day at the zoo. They had seen their favourite animals and lots more.

'Can we come to the zoo again tomorrow?' asked Hattie on the way home.

'Well, maybe another day,' mummy said.